This Bing book belongs to:

. . . .

First published in Great Britain in 2014 by HarperCollins *Children's Books*,
a division of HarperCollins *Publishers* Ltd, 1 London Bridge Street, London, SE1 9GF

3 5 7 9 10 8 6 4 2

ISBN: 978-0-00-797946-2

Based on the script by Lead Writers: Ted Dewan and Philip Bergkvist and Team Writers: Lucy Murphy and Mikael Shields.

Adapted from the original books by Ted Dewan and using images created by Acamar Films, Brown Bag Films and Tandem Ltd.

Edited by Neil Dunnicliffe.

Designed by Anna Lubecka.

www.harpercollins.co.uk

Printed in China

Bing and Flop are
in the kitchen.
It's snack-time
for Bing.

Flop takes
a carrot.

He **spins** it,
throws it up
into the air...

and
catch
it

Yum!

Bing **loves** carrots.

He takes a
big bite.

CRUNNCH!

Bing **throws** the carrot in the air.

WHOOPS!

Where did it go?

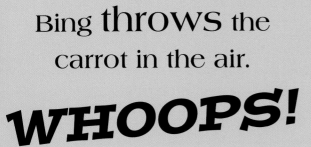

There
it is!

Now it's time for **milk** and a **banana**.
Flop pulls the last banana out of the bowl.

Oh dear, it's **very ripe**
and **very brown**.

"Yuk! It's mushy. I don't want to eat it," Bing says.

"Why don't we **drink** the banana?" asks Flop.

"Silly Flop, you can't **drink** a banana!" laughs Bing.

"You can't drink a banana?"
says Flop as he brings in...

Brenda the blender!

"Brenda the blender. Food blender extra-ordin-aire. Let's make a smoothie," says Flop.

"Can I do **top speed?**" asks Bing.

"Sure. But first we have to **squish** the banana into the jug, fill the jug with milk, mix it up at low speed and then..."

"**Top speed!**" shouts Bing.

Bing **squeezes** the banana out of its skin.

"It's doing a poo!" he giggles.

PLOP!

PLOP!

PLOP!

It drops into the blender.

"Now let's add the milk," says Flop.

"Low speed first. To get the lumps out. If it's lumpy, you know what happens? Brenda goes

wubble,

wubble,

wubble!"

"Ok... let's go...go...go...go...go!"

Brenda mixes everything together.
"All the lumps are gone, but we need to add a
little more milk," says Flop.

Bing isn't listening. He's **throwing** his carrot.

WHOOPS!

Where did it go?

Flop adds more milk to the blender and puts the lid back on.

"OK, Bing. Top speed?" he says.

"Yup. **Top speed!**" shouts Bing.

"Let's go...go...go...go...go!"

Brenda **shakes** and takes
a while to reach top speed.

Suddenly Bing **wonders**
where his carrot has gone.

Then he **spots**
something inside
the blender.

"Brenda's got
my carrot!"
says Bing. "I want
my carrot!"

Flop looks inside the blender. "I don't think your carrot is going to come back," he says.

"Whhhyyyyy?"
asks Bing.

"Because the banana,
the milk and your carrot
are all mixed up together.

LOOK!" says Flop,
"Brenda's made you
a yummy carrot
smoothie."

"Try it, Bing!"

Bing sips the
smoothie through
a straw.

"Aaahhh."

"Yum?"

"Ooh,
yum!"

"Good for you, Bing Bunny."

Hi!

My banana was all **mushy**.

So we put the **pooey** banana and the milk into Brenda, and Brenda **mixed** everything together.

But Brenda took my carrot and that was **naughty.**

And my carrot wouldn't come out, so we made a **carrot smoothie.**

It was yummy delicious!

You can mix things up, but you can't mix them down again.

Making a smoothie...

it's a Bing thing.